P9-CQE-411

For Mary Vazquez—L. N.

To all the little piggies in my life—E. O.

SIMON & SCHUSTER BOOKS FOR YOUNG READERS
An imprint of Simon & Schuster Children's Publishing Division
1230 Avenue of the Americas, New York, New York 10020
Text copyright © 2003 by Lesléa Newman
Illustrations copyright © 2003 by Erika Oller
All rights reserved, including the right of reproduction in whole or in part in any form.
SIMON & SCHUSTER BOOKS FOR YOUNG READERS is a trademark of Simon & Schuster.
Book design by Greg Stadnyk
The text of this book is set in Clearface.
The illustrations are rendered in watercolor.
Manufactured in China
2 4 6 8 10 9 7 5 3 1
Library of Congress Cataloging-in-Publication Data
Newman, Lesléa.
Pigs, pigs, pigs! / by Lesléa Newman ; illustrated by Erika Oller.—1st ed.
p. cm.
Summary: A town prepares for and enjoys a visit with a large group of very entertaining pigs in this rhyming tale of hospitality.
ISBN 0-689-84979-6
[1. Pigs—Fiction. 2. Hospitality—Fiction. 3. Entertainers—Fiction. 4. Stories in rhyme.] I. Oller, Erika, ill. II. Title.
PZ8.3.N4655 Pi 2003
[E]—dc21
2001042847

Pigs, Pigs, Pigs!

by
LESLÉA NEWMAN

illustrated by
ERIKA OLLER

Simon & Schuster Books for Young Readers

New York   London   Toronto   Sydney   Singapore

The pigs are coming to play, hooray!
The pigs are coming today.
We'd better take care to completely prepare,
A minute's too long to delay.

WELCOME PIGGIES!
ALL ABOUT PIGS
To Live Like a Pig
Dining with Pigs

They're coming by bus and by train and by plane,

They're coming by hot-air balloon.

They're coming by yak and by pink Cadillac,

They're coming, they'll be here by noon.

We're planning a feast for ten thousand at least,
We're cooking a fabulous meal.

We're mixing and baking and fixing and making
A spread that will make those pigs squeal:

Fried green tomatoes and mashed sweet potatoes,
Troughs full of twice-baked spaghetti.

Cheese tortellini with deep-fried zucchini,
And buckets of Apple Brown Betty.

Gooey chop suey that tastes rather chewy,
Pastrami with mustard on rye,

Mountains of chips served with fountains of dips,
And coconut chocolate cream pie.

The pigs are quite near, oh my dear, they are here!
See our mayor embracing the sows.

"This way to the party. Please come and eat hearty."
She grins ear to ear as she bows.

The pigs sit politely but hardly eat lightly.
In fact they all pig out in style.

They munch and they crunch on
their oversized lunch,
Then each one sits back with a smile.

"The feast was quite yummy." A pig pats his tummy.
"Thank you so much for the treat.

And now as you know it is time for the show."
And with that the pigs leap to their feet.

They sing and they dance and they swing and they prance,
They light up the stage like the sun.

Our hands get to clapping, our feet set to tapping,
And then we all join in the fun.

Each grown-up and child
goes completely hog-wild
As the pigs kick their heels
to the roofs.

We wiggle and whirl as they jiggle and twirl
On their thundering, delicate hoofs.

After the show the pigs say they must go,
But first may they please have a snack?

We offer them plum cakes and rum cakes and crumb cakes,
And beg them to please hurry back.

We're tired and weary, in fact we're quite bleary,
But none of us can fall asleep.

We've got to hold steady, we've got to get ready,
Our next guests are coming—the sheep!

DISCARDED

PEACHTREE

J PICTURE NEWMAN

Newman, Lesléa.
   Pigs, pigs, pigs!

Atlanta-Fulton Public Library

JUL 07 2003